THE USBORNE BOOK OF
EARTH FACTS

Lynn Bresler

P9-BYL-279

CONTENTS

Designed by Teresa Foster

**Illustrated by Tony Gibson
and Ian Jackson**

With thanks to Chris Rice and Stephen Capus

Earth's vital statistics

Earth's place in the Universe

Our galaxy is one of 400 million galaxies in the Universe. The small part of our galaxy which you can see in the sky is called the Milky Way. It contains over 3,000 million stars. If each star was a full stop, like this, . . . they would make a line stretching from London to Moscow.

Earth statistics

Diameter:	
at the Poles	12,713 km
at the Equator	12,756 km
Circumference:	
round the Poles	40,000 km
round the Equator	40,075 km
Density:	5.518g/cm^3
Volume:	1.08×10^{12} km^3

Total surface area: 510,066,000 sq km
Weight: 6,000 million million million tonnes

The solar system

The Sun is one of the stars in the Milky Way. Nine planets revolve around it. Scientists think the Sun and planets were all formed about 4,600 million years ago.

The Earth's Moon

The Earth is the third nearest planet to the Sun. It has one natural satellite orbiting it, the Moon, which is 384,365 km (238,840 miles) from the Earth. The Moon is a quarter the size of the Earth.

The short way round

The Earth is not a true sphere. It is slightly flattened at the top and bottom. The diameter through the Poles is 43 km (26 miles) less than it is at the Equator.

Watery Earth

About 70 per cent of the Earth's surface is covered in water. The southern hemisphere is more watery than the northern hemisphere. Over 80 per cent of the people on Earth live north of the Equator.

The Continents

Continent	Area in sq km
Asia	44,391,200
Africa	30,244,000
North America	24,247,000
South America	17,821,000
Antarctica	13,338,500
Europe	10,354,600
Oceania	8,547,000

Faraway

The 299 people on Tristan da Cunha, in the Atlantic Ocean, live on the most isolated inhabited island on Earth. Their nearest neighbours are on the island of St Helena, 2,120 km (1,320 miles) away.

Bouvey Oya, in the South Atlantic Ocean, is the most isolated uninhabited island on Earth. It is 1,700 km (1,050 miles) from the east coast of Antarctica.

Largest islands	
Island	Area in sq km
Greenland	2,175,000
New Guinea	789,900
Borneo	751,000
Madagascar	587,000
Baffin	507,400
Sumatra	422,200
Honshu	230,000
Great Britain	229,800
Victoria	217,300
Ellesmere	196,200

New land

New islands are still being formed by volcanoes erupting under the sea. Surtsey emerged from the sea off the coast of Iceland in 1963. The newest island is Lateiki, off the east coast of Australia, which was first spotted in 1979.

Surtsey

DID YOU KNOW?

The Pacific Ocean, the largest ocean, is three times bigger than Asia, the largest continent.

Inside the Earth

The surface of the Earth is a thin crust of rock. Under this, scientists believe, is a layer of liquid rock, the mantle, which surrounds an outer core of liquid iron and nickel. The inner core at the centre of the Earth is probably a solid ball of iron and nickel.

Inside the Earth statistics

Layer	Depth in km	Layer	Temperature
Crust under sea	8	Crust	21°C average
Crust under land	40	Mantle	1500-3000°C
Mantle	2,870	Outer core	3900°C
Outer core	2,100	Inner core	4000°C
Inner core	1,370 (radius)		

The Earth's history

In the beginning

Scientists think that the Earth was formed, about 4,600 million years ago, from a spinning cloud of dust and gases, which shrank to a hot, molten globe. As this cooled, a crust of rock formed on the surface. The oldest of the Earth's rocks are in west Greenland, and are 3,820 million years old.

Jigsaw

The crust of the Earth is not one solid piece. It is cracked into a jigsaw of 7 huge pieces, and several smaller ones. The pieces, called plates, are about 64 km (40 miles) thick. The plates float on the hot, liquid rock of the mantle, the deep layer beneath the crust.

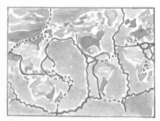

Bump! Crunch!

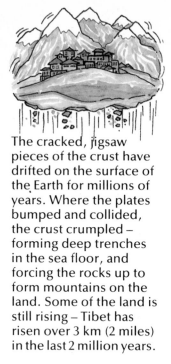

The cracked, jigsaw pieces of the crust have drifted on the surface of the Earth for millions of years. Where the plates bumped and collided, the crust crumpled – forming deep trenches in the sea floor, and forcing the rocks up to form mountains on the land. Some of the land is still rising – Tibet has risen over 3 km (2 miles) in the last 2 million years.

Slip sliding away

The plates can slip past each other on land, as well as under the sea. The San Andreas Fault, in the USA, a boundary between 2 plates, is a great crack, stretching for 1,126 km (700 miles) from the Gulf of California. Over 15 million years, California has moved about 300 km (186 miles) north-westwards, and in 50 million years' time, might have split away.

The changing crust

New crust is being made all the time on the sea floor. Hot, liquid rock bubbles up through the huge cracks between the plates, such as the ridge in the middle of the Atlantic Ocean. As much as 10 cm (4 in) of new rock a year can be formed, on either side of the crack.

The ridge is close to the surface underneath Iceland. The island is expanding very slowly, where liquid rock spills out from great cracks which run across the island.

In other places on the sea floor, the plates slide over each other. This forces some of the crust down deep sea trenches, such as the Peru-Chile Trench in the Pacific Ocean, back into the hot mantle.

Continental drift

The drifting of the Earth's crust means the continents have not always been in the same place. North Africa was once covered in a sheet of ice and was where the South Pole is today. And the South Pole was once covered with rain forests.

Yesterday

About 200 million years ago, most of the land was probably joined up into a large continent, called Pangaea. This split into two – Laurasia, now mainly in the northern hemisphere, and Gondwanaland, now mainly in the southern.

Today

The continents are still moving today. In 50 million years' time, Alaska and the USSR may have joined together.

Tomorrow?

Wearing away

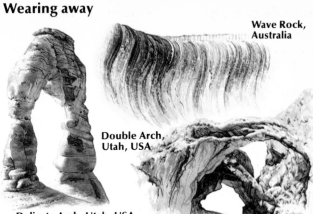

Wave Rock, Australia

Double Arch, Utah, USA

Delicate Arch, Utah, USA

The landscape has changed over millions of years. Erosion by ice, wind and water has worn away the surface of the Earth. Glaciers have carved valleys, fjords and jagged mountain peaks. Rivers have carved great canyons, such as the Grand Canyon in Colorado, USA, which is 349 km (217 miles) long. Rain and wind have sculpted cliffs, such as Wave Rock in Australia, and natural arches, such as Delicate Arch, in Utah, USA.

All change!

The people on Earth have changed the landscape too. They have cleared forests, straightened rivers, and terraced steep hillsides for farming. They have quarried rocks, metals and minerals out of the ground. The Bingham Canyon copper mine in Utah, USA, has created a hole 3.7 km (2.3 miles) across and 789 m (2,590 ft) deep. People have also created new land, by reclaiming land from the sea, such as one-third of the farm land in The Netherlands.

The Earth's atmosphere

Outside the Earth

The Earth is surrounded by a blanket of air, called the atmosphere, which is divided into different layers. The highest reaches up into Space, 8,000 km (5,000 miles) above the Earth.

In the beginning

The Earth's atmosphere was originally a hot, steamy mixture of gases. Scientists think that it was made up of gases such as methane, nitrogen, hydrogen and carbon dioxide, as well as water vapour.

DID YOU KNOW?

There is enough water in the atmosphere, that if it all fell as rain at the same time, it would cover the entire surface of the Earth with 2.5 cm (1 in) of water.

Oxygen – the air that we breathe

Oxygen was first formed only about 2,000 million years ago, when plants, called algae, started to appear on the Earth. Plants produce oxygen in sunlight, which animals, including people, breathe in. All animals breathe out carbon dioxide, which plants breathe in.

Gasping for air

The higher you go, the thinner the air, which is why mountaineers need extra oxygen. The density of air at the top of Everest is only about one-third that at sea level.

Atmospheric heights

Layer	Height above Earth
Exosphere	500-8,000 km
Thermosphere	80-500 km
Mesosphere	50-80 km
Stratosphere	8-50 km
Troposphere (over Equator)	16 km
(over Poles)	8 km

What is the atmosphere made of?

The highest layer, the exosphere, is probably made mostly of helium, hydrogen and oxygen.

The lower layers are made of:

Gas	Per cent
Nitrogen	75.51
Oxygen	23.15
Argon	1.28
Carbon dioxide	
Neon	
Helium	
Krypton	.06
Hydrogen	
Xenon	
Ozone	

Plus water vapour, and microscopic dust particles, plant spores and pollen grain

Atmospheric temperatures

Layer	Temperature
Exosphere	2200°C minimum
Thermosphere	−80°C to 2,200°C
Mesosphere	10°C to −80°C
Stratosphere	−55°C to 10°C
Troposphere	
(at 16 km high)	−55°C
(at sea level)	15°C

Bouncing waves

Radio signals move at the speed of light, 300,000 km (186,420 miles) per second. The signals can travel around the curve of the Earth, by bouncing off the electrically-charged air in the mesosphere and thermosphere.

Flying high

The troposphere is the storm, wind and cloud layer. Planes fly high above the weather, in the stratosphere, where they use air currents, called jet streams, which can blow at up to 483 km (300 miles) per hour. Most of the jet streams blow from west to east.

Dust high

A giant volcanic eruption can throw dust and ash as high as the stratosphere. The dust and ash can travel halfway around the world, and take as long as three years to fall back to Earth.

Force of gravity

The atmosphere is held to the Earth by the force of gravity. Astronauts have to travel through the atmosphere at more than 27,360 km (17,000 miles) per hour to break free of Earth's gravity.

Sunscreen

Up in the stratosphere, 24 km (15 miles) above the Earth, is the ozone layer. This filters out the Sun's harmful ultra-violet rays – without the ozone, life would not survive on Earth.

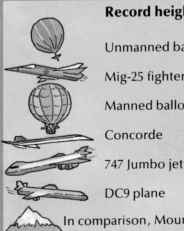

Record heights	Height above Earth
Unmanned balloon	52 km
Mig-25 fighter plane	38 km
Manned balloon	35 km
Concorde	18 km
747 Jumbo jet	12 km
DC9 plane	8 km

In comparison, Mount Everest is 9 km high.

Mountains

High ground

About 25 per cent of the Earth's land surface is 914 m (3,000 ft) or more above sea level. Of this, most of the continent of Antarctica is about 1,829 m (6,000 ft) high and the country of Tibet averages 4,572 m (15,000 ft) high.

Capital fact

The highest capital city in the world is La Paz, in Bolivia. It is 3,625 m (11,893 ft) up in the Andes.

Avalanche!

The slam of a car door, a falling branch or the movement of a skier can start an avalanche. The snow can slide down at a speed of 322 km (200 miles) an hour.

High living

There is less oxygen the higher up you go. Mountain people and animals can live at great heights because they have bigger hearts and lungs, which carry more blood, and therefore more oxygen.

Quechua Indians live 3,650 m (12,000 ft) up in the Andes, where they grow potatoes and corn, and herd sheep.

Mountain heights

People and wildlife can survive at different heights up a mountain. This shows some of the life of the Himalayas.

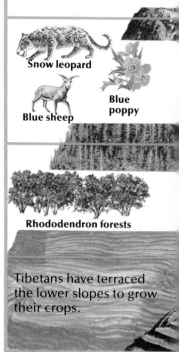

Snow leopard

Blue sheep

Blue poppy

Rhododendron forests

Tibetans have terraced the lower slopes to grow their crops.

Cliff climbers

Rocky Mountain goats can climb up cliffs which are almost vertical. Tough pads on their hooves act as suction cups, and stop them from slipping on the steep rocks.

Highest mountain by continent

Continent	Location	Mountain	Height
Asia	Nepal/Tibet	Everest	8,848 m
Africa	Tanzania	Kilimanjaro	5,895 m
North America	Alaska	McKinley	6,194 m
South America	Argentina	Aconcagua	6,960 m
Antarctica	Ellsworth Land	Vinson Massif	5,140 m
Western Europe	France	Mont Blanc	4,810 m
Eastern Europe	USSR	Elbrus	5,633 m
Oceania	New Zealand	Cook	3,764 m

7,600 m (25,000 ft)

Springtail   Alpine chough

Jumping spider Cushion pinks

4,900 m (16,000 ft)

Tibetans take their yaks up as high as 4,600 m (15,000 ft) to graze during the summer.

3,000 m (10,000 ft)

Red panda   Asian black bear

1,200 m (4,000 ft)

Longest mountain ranges

Range	Location	Length
Andes	South America	7,240 km
Rockies	North America	6,030 km
Himalaya/Karakoram/Hindu Kush	Asia	3,860 km
Great Dividing Range	Australia	3,620 km
Trans-Antarctic	Antarctica	3,540 km

The Andes are over twice as long as North America is wide.

Mountain climate

The higher you go up a mountain, the colder it gets. The temperature drops by 2°C (3.6°F) for every 300 m (984 ft) of height. The temperature is as low as −20°C (−4°F) at the top of the Himalayas, where fierce winds can reach over 300 km (186 miles) an hour.

DID YOU KNOW?

Seashells can be found in rocks high up on some mountains, such as the Apennines in Italy. The rocks were once at the bottom of the sea. They were pushed upwards over millions of years, as the crust of the Earth crumpled.

Changing shape

As they get older, mountains gradually change shape. Frost and ice split and wear away the rock. Scientists think mountains lose about 8.6 cm (3½ in) every 1,000 years.

Mountain ages

Mountain ranges are millions of years old, but they are not all the same age.

Scientists have worked out the approximate age of mountain ranges. Here are some examples.

Million years old	Location	Mountain range
400	Scotland	Highlands
250	USA	Appalachians
	USSR	Urals
80	South America	Andes
70	North America	Rockies
40	Asia	Himalayas
15	Europe	Alps

Tundra

Frozen prairie

The frozen prairie, the flat tundra, stretches between the tree line (the northern edge of forest lands) and the Arctic polar region. It is almost 1½ times the size of Brazil, covering nearly one-tenth of the Earth's land surface, including northern Canada, Norway, Sweden, Finland and Greenland, Siberia, Alaska and Iceland.

Soggy landscape

The tundra has only about 20 cm (8 in) of rain a year. The permafrost stops the water from draining away, so about half the area of tundra is dotted with marshes and shallow lakes. Only the top few cms of tundra thaw each summer.

Northern dawn

The ghostly lights of the Aurora borealis shimmer and glow high in the atmosphere in the far north. Curtains and streamers of light move across the winter skies.

Tundra people

About 90,000 Eskimos live in the tundra area. Most of them now live in wooden houses, but in Greenland and Canada, a few still live in igloos. Other tundra dwellers include 300,000 Yakuts in Siberia and 30,000 Lapps in Scandinavia.

Commuter caribou

Herds of caribou, as many as 100,000 in each herd, trek 600 km (373 miles) north to the tundra every spring, where the young caribou are born. As summer ends, they return south, following routes they have used for centuries.

Amazing But True

Scientists were able to make a 10,000-year-old seed germinate and sprout. The Arctic lupin seed was found in Yukon, in Canada.

Tundra statistics	
Area of tundra	13,000,000 sq km
Depth of permafrost	305-610 m
Temperature	
Winter	−29 to −34°C
Summer	3 to 12°C

Winter white

Many of the birds and animals which live on the tundra all year round change colour according to the season. In autumn they turn white to match the snow; in spring, they change back to their summer colours.

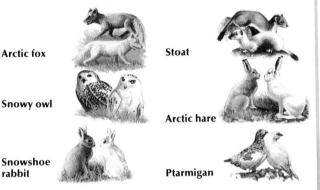

Arctic fox

Snowy owl

Snowshoe rabbit

Stoat

Arctic hare

Ptarmigan

DID YOU KNOW?

The Trans-Alaskan oil pipeline stretches 1,300 km (800 miles) from the Arctic Ocean to southern Alaska. The oil is heated to at least 45°C (130°F), to stop it freezing in the pipe.

Buzz off!

In calm weather, during the short summer, plagues of mosquitoes and other flies infest the tundra. Warble flies are so ferocious, they can cause madness in some of the caribou herds.

Deep freeze

The permafrost can act as a deep freeze. Ice Age mammoths have been found in Siberia. And the body of John Torrington, a British naval officer who died in 1845, on an expedition to the Bering Strait, was found in 1983.

Colder than ice

In the winter, under its blanket of ice and snow, the tundra in north-east Siberia is colder, at −70°C (−94°F), than it is at the North Pole.

Permafrost

The permafrost, the deep layer of ground beneath the tundra, is frozen all the year round. A layer as much as 1,500 m (4,921 ft) deep has been recorded in Siberia.

Low life

You can walk on top of the tundra forests. Near to the tree line, the trees are so blasted by the cold, dry winds, they grow close to the ground. Branches of ground willow can be up to 5 m (16 ft) in length, but they only rise above the surface by about 10 cm (4 in).

Forests . . . 1

Coniferous trees

Coniferous trees have cones and needle-like leaves. Most conifers are evergreen, but some, such as larches, lose their needles in the autumn. Coniferous forests grow in colder climates in the far north, and high up on mountains – even those in the Tropics.

Broad-leaved trees

Broad-leaved trees have flowers and wide, flat leaves. Some broad-leaved trees are deciduous, they lose their leaves in autumn; others are evergreen. Deciduous broad-leaved forests grow in warm, temperate climates. Evergreen broad-leaved forests grow where it is hot and wet all the time.

Forest statistics

Coniferous forests stretch across northern Europe, Asia and North America, and are found in mountain regions, such as the Rockies, Alps and Urals. Mixed and deciduous broad-leaved forests are found mostly in west and central Europe, eastern USA, and parts of Japan, China and New Zealand.

Type of forest	Type of trees
Coniferous	Conifers
Mixed	Deciduous broad-leaved/ conifers
Deciduous	Deciduous broad-leaved
Tropical rain	Evergreen broad-leaved

The tropical rain forests equal all the other forest types added together.

Timber merchant

Coniferous trees supply almost three-quarters of the world's timber, as well as nearly all the paper used. It takes one tree to produce 270 copies of a 190-page paperback book.

Rooted deep

Hickory trees grow to 37 m (120 ft) tall. The main root, the taproot, could be as long as 30 m (100 ft) – the root may be nearly as deep as the tree is high.

Coniferous forest trees

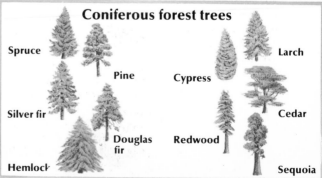

Spruce
Pine
Silver fir
Douglas fir
Hemlock
Cypress
Redwood
Larch
Cedar
Sequoia

Deciduous broad-leaved forest trees

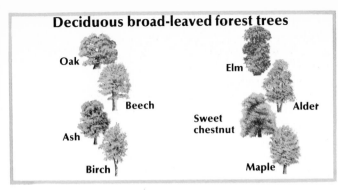

Oak

Beech

Ash

Birch

Elm

Sweet chestnut

Alder

Maple

Oldest, largest, tallest

The mountain forests of north-west America have the oldest and the largest and the tallest trees on Earth.

Bristlecone pines nearly 5,000 years old, about the same age as the Pyramids in Egypt. Giant sequoias up to 7.6 m (26 ft) across - wide enough to drive a car through. Redwoods up to 107 m (350 ft) tall. Four balanced on top of each other would be nearly as high as the Sears Roebuck Tower, the world's tallest building.

Fire-proof trees

Fires can burn forests at a rate of up to 15 km (10 miles) an hour, and the roar of the fire can be heard 1.6 km (1 mile) away. Trees protected by very thick bark, for example pine and sequoia, are only scarred by the fire, the wood is undamaged.

Woodlands

Woodland flowers bloom in the spring, before the trees come into leaf and block most of the sunlight. When the leaves fall in autumn they rot, forming humus, which makes the soil more fertile.

Crops from coniferous trees

Part of tree	Some examples of use
Timber	Furniture
	Matches
	Tannic acid
Pulp	Paper
	Plastics
	Rayon
Cellulose	Cellophane
	Turpentine
Needles	Pine-leaf oil (used in soap)
	Vitamins A and E

Amazing But True

Each year, every person in the USA uses up enough items made from wood to equal a tree 30 m (100 ft) tall and 41 cm (16 in) in diameter. That adds up to over 230 million trees a year.

Giant cone

The largest pine cones grow on the sugar pine trees of the USA. They reach 66 cm (26 in) long, nearly two-thirds the length of a baseball bat.

Forests . . . 2

Tropical rain forests

Rain forests cover about 6 per cent of the Earth's land surface. A hundred million years ago, rain forests grew in Norway. Today, they are mostly on or south of the Equator, for example in New Guinea, Malaysia and parts of Africa, Burma, Indonesia and South America.

Treeless forests

Great forests of bamboo, over 18 m (60 ft) high, grow in the south-western mountains of China, where giant pandas live. Bamboo is not a tree, it is a type of grass. Field grass grows to an average of only 100 cm (39 in).

Flying frogs

Asian tree frogs (10 cm, 4 in long) can "fly" from one tree to another, as much as 12 m (40 ft) away. The webs of skin between their toes act as parachutes.

DID YOU KNOW?

About 2,500 million people, half the world's population, use wood for cooking and heating.

Daily rain

It rains nearly every day in the tropical rain forests. At least 203 cm (80 in) and as much as 381 cm (150 in) can fall each year. The temperature rarely drops below 26.6°C (80°F) and the air is 80 per cent moisture.

Rain forest layers

The plants and trees in the tropical rain forests grow up to different heights. The forest can be divided into five "layers".

Layer	Height
Attic	up to 91 m
Canopy	46-76 m
Understorey	6-12 m
Shrub	0.6-6 m
Herb	up to 0.6 m

Slowcoach

In the forests of South America is the slowest moving land mammal. The sloth spends much of its time hanging upside-down from trees. When it does move, it creeps along at 2 m (7 ft) a minute.

Bush ropes

Bush ropes, or lianas, hang down from the rain forest canopy. They can be 60 cm (2 ft) thick and as much as 152 m (500 ft) long, and are strong enough to swing on.

Perching plants

Perching plants grow on trees high up in the canopy, where they absorb food and moisture from the air. Plants, such as bromeliads, can provide a home for insects and frogs, 70 m (230 ft) above the forest floor.

Life in the rain forest

Only 1 per cent of sunlight reaches the rain forest floor. So most of the insects, birds and animals have to live up in the canopy, where there is more sunlight and food.

Tree kangaroos live in the New Guinea forests. They mostly live up in the trees, but can jump down to the forest floor from a height of 18 m (59 ft). Their tails are longer than their bodies.

Rain forest crops

The Earth's rain forests supply many of our crops. Rubber, lacquer, gum, waxes and dyes can all be made from rain forest trees. Here are some other examples.

Timber	Mahogany
	Teak
Fruit	Bananas
	Pineapples
Spices	Paprika
	Pepper
Oils	Palm
	Patchouli
Fibres	Jute
	Rattan
Beans	Coffee
	Cocoa

Cloud forest giants

Giant plants grow 3,000 m (9,842 ft) up in the cloud forests on Mount Kenya, where the trees are blanketed in fog and mist. Groundsel, over 6 m (20 ft) high, look like giant cabbages on trunks. Lobelias, up to 8 m (26 ft) tall, look like furry columns because of their hairy leaves.

Medicine cabinet

Some of our medicines are made from rain forest trees. Quinine and aspirin are made from tree bark; cough mixture is made from tree resin.

Lakes and rivers

Drop of water

Only 3 per cent of all the water on Earth is fresh; the rest is salty. Of that 3 per cent, over 2 per cent is frozen in ice sheets and glaciers; so less than 1 per cent is in lakes, rivers and under the ground.

Continent	Country	River	Length
Asia	China	Yangtze	5,520 km
Africa	Egypt	Nile	6,670 km
North America	USA	Mississippi/ Missouri	6,020 km
South America	Brazil	Amazon	6,437 km
Eastern Europe	USSR	Volga	3,688 km
Western Europe	Germany	Rhine	1,320 km
Oceania	Australia	Murray/Darling	3,720 km

Longest rivers by continent

Some of the rivers flow through more than one country. Most of each river is in the country listed.

DID YOU KNOW?

Not all rivers end up in an ocean. The rivers flowing south from the Tassili Mountains in north Africa, slow down to a trickle and disappear into the dry Sahara sands.

Deepest lake

Lake Baikal, in the USSR, is 644 km (400 miles) long and 48 km (30 miles) wide. It is so deep, ranging from 1,620-1,940 m (5,315-6,365 ft), that all five of the Great Lakes in North America could be emptied into it.

Amazing But True

Piranhas are ferocious, flesh-eating fish. Their triangular teeth are so sharp, the Amazonian Indians use them as scissors.

Living afloat

One of the highest lakes is Titicaca, 3,810 m (12,500 ft) up in the Peruvian Andes. There are "floating" islands on the lake, some as big as football fields, made from thickly matted totora reeds. People live on the islands, and build their houses, boats and baskets from the reeds – and they eat the roots of the reeds too.

Highest waterfalls

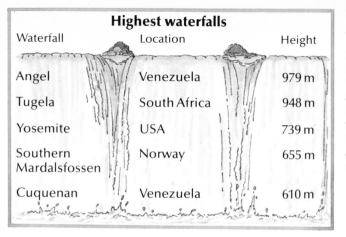

Waterfall	Location	Height
Angel	Venezuela	979 m
Tugela	South Africa	948 m
Yosemite	USA	739 m
Southern Mardalsfossen	Norway	655 m
Cuquenan	Venezuela	610 m

The mighty Amazon

The Amazon is the greatest river on Earth. It starts 5,200 m (17,000 ft) up in the snows of the Andes, and ends 6,437 km (4,000 miles) later on the Atlantic coast, in a maze of islands and channels, 300 km (186 miles) wide.

Niagara on the move

Niagara Falls are midway along the Niagara River, which flows between Lakes Ontario and Erie. The Falls date back 10,000 years, to the end of the last Ice Age.

At that time they were 11 km (7 miles) further downriver; the pounding water has gradually worn away the rocks at the edge of the Falls. In about 25,000 years' time, Niagara will disappear when the Falls reach Lake Erie – and the Lake may drain away.

Busy waterfall

The Iguazu Falls in Brazil are 4 km (2½ miles) wide and 80 m (260 ft) high. During the rainy season, November to March, the amount of water pouring over the Falls every second would fill about 6 Olympic-size swimming pools.

The Amazon's flow of water is so great, one-fifth of all river water, that the freshwater stretches 180 km (112 miles) out to sea, colouring the sea with yellow-brown silt.

Largest lakes and inland seas

Most lakes contain freshwater, but two of the largest – the Aral and the Caspian – are really inland seas, as they contain saltwater.

Lake/inland sea	Location	Size
Caspian Sea	Iran/USSR	372,000 sq km
Superior	Canada/USA	82,414 sq km
Victoria	East Africa	69,485 sq km
Aral Sea	USSR	66,500 sq km
Huron	Canada/USA	59,596 sq km
Michigan	USA	58,016 sq km
Tanganyika	East Africa	32,893 sq km

Grasslands and savannahs

Grassy places

Grasslands and savannahs cover about one-quarter of the land on Earth. Savannahs have patches of grass, up to 4.5 m (15 ft) tall, and scrub, bushes and a few small trees. Grasslands can be used for growing crops, such as wheat, or as pasture, for grazing animals. The grass height ranges from 30-215 cm (1-7 ft).

Indian grass

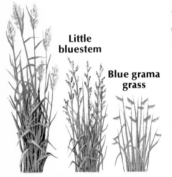

Little bluestem

Blue grama grass

Grassy names

Grasslands and savannahs are called different names in different parts of the world. These are some examples.

Grasslands

Country	Name
Argentina	Pampas
North America	Prairie
South Africa	Veldt
Central Asia	Steppes
Australia	Scrub

Savannahs

Country	Name
East Africa	Savannah
Brazil	Campo
Venezuela	Llanos

DID YOU KNOW?

The largest wheatfield, in Alberta, Canada, covered an area of 142 sq km (55 sq miles). That added up to nearly 20,000 soccer pitches.

Grasslands

There are grasslands in Europe, Asia, North America, South America, South Africa and Australia in areas where there is too little rain for forests to grow, but enough rain to stop the land turning to desert.

Grasslands have hot summers and cold winters. In the North American prairies, the temperature in winter can drop to freezing (0°C, 32°F) and climb to 38°C (100°F) in summer. Rainfall can vary between 50-100 cm (20-40 in) a year.

All about grasses

There are about 10,000 different kinds of grass on Earth. Most grasses have hollow stems, although some have solid stems, such as maize and sugar cane.

Grasses are flowering plants, but are pollinated by the wind carrying pollen from flower to flower. So grasses do not need brightly coloured flowers to attract insects to carry the pollen.

New grass

Grass fires, which can be sparked off by lightning, can destroy grass stems, but the grass soon grows back again. The growing point of grass is so close to the ground, at the base of the leaves, that it does not get burnt – or even eaten by animals as they graze the grass.

Crops

Cereal crops have been developed by people from wild grasses. They are used as food for people and for animals. Here are some examples.

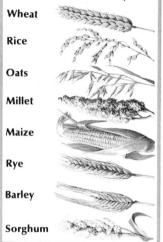

Wheat

Rice

Oats

Millet

Maize

Rye

Barley

Sorghum

Savannah choice

Different animals on the savannah eat different plants. Giraffes feed on branches high in trees; antelopes feed on lower branches. Zebras eat the tops of grasses; wildebeest eat the rest of the stem; and gazelles eat the young shoots.

Rice

Rice is the only grass which can grow in water, and is the main food of more than half the world's population. Almost all of the rice – about 90 per cent – is grown in Asia.

Upside-down trees

The baobab trees of Africa have enormous, swollen trunks, in which water is stored, topped by short, stumpy branches which look more like tree roots. Old trees are sometimes hollow, and have been used as bus shelters – or even as houses.

Savannahs

Savannahs are mostly near the Equator, in Africa, South-East Asia and India, and in Australia, in areas where it is warm all the year round. Some savannahs are dry for as much as 10 months of the year, with only 20 cm (8 in) of rain. Others are dry for only 3 months, with as much as 120 cm (47 in) of rain.

Staying alive

The colours of animals living in savannahs help to protect them from predators, but also hides the predators themselves. Striped or spotted animals, such as cheetahs and leopards, are difficult to see from a distance, especially when they move through sunlight and shadow. The tawny colour of a lion hides it in the long, dry grass.

Deserts

What is a desert?

A desert is an area which has less than 25 cm (10 in) of rain a year, and very little plant life. In some deserts, the total rain for the year might fall in only two or three storms. But that is enough for plant seeds to sprout and bloom, turning parts of the desert into carpets of flowers for a few days.

Largest deserts		
Desert	Location	Size in sq km
Sahara	North Africa	8,400,000
Australian	Australia	1,550,000
Arabian	South-West Asia	1,300,000
Gobi	Central Asia	1,040,000
Patagonia	South America	670,000
Kalahari	Southern Africa	520,000
Turkestan	Central Asia	450,000
Takla Makan	China	320,000
Sonoran	USA/Mexico	310,000
Namib	South-West Africa	310,000

Deserted places

Deserts cover about 20 per cent of the Earth's land surface. Many desert areas are bare rock, or are covered with pebbles and gravel. Sand accounts for only about 15 per cent of the Earth's desert regions.

Colossal cacti

Cacti are found only in American deserts. The tallest are saguaros which can reach 15 m (50 ft) tall, weigh 7 tons and live for 200 years. Water is stored in the stem and used in times of drought.

The driest land

The Atacama in northern Chile is the driest desert on Earth. Parts of the desert had no rain for 400 years, from 1570-1971, and in other parts, rain has never been recorded.

Death Valley

WATER 100KM

At 57°C (134°F), Death Valley is the driest, hottest place in North America. Gold prospectors died there, in 1849, when they ran out of food and water on their way to the Californian goldfields – which is how the Valley got its name.

Sandstorm

One of the sandiest deserts is the Takla Makan. Sandstorms can whip up the sand as high as 3,048 m (10,000 ft). Wind-blown sand in the Sahara can be so fierce, it will sandblast the paint off a car or aeroplane.

Hot and cold deserts

There are 10 major desert regions. "Cold" deserts have hot summers and relatively cold winters. "Hot" deserts are hot during the day, all the year round.

Cold deserts
West/south-west North
  America
Patagonia
Turkestan
Gobi

Hot deserts
Sahara
Namib/Kalahari
Arabian
Iranian
Atacama
Australian

Sahara

The Sahara is almost one-third the size of Africa, and is nearly as big as the USA, the fourth largest country. It was not always a desert. Over millions of years it has been covered in ice, sea, forests and grasslands.

Moving dunes

Sand dunes move. The wind blows the sand up one side of the dune, and some of the sand trickles over the top and slips down the other side. Dunes creep forward between 10 and 50 m (33 to 164 ft) a year, and can engulf villages and oases.

Temperature

The temperature at night in a hot desert can drop below freezing, to −4°C (24°F). During the day, the sand can be as hot as 79°C (175°F).

Desert snow

Each year, a thin layer of snow (5 cm, 2 in) blankets the cacti in many North American deserts. And snow sometimes falls on the Ahaggar Mountains in the Sahara Desert.

Desert dinosaurs

Dinosaurs once lived in the Gobi Desert in Asia. Fossilized eggs and bones have been found there, and the skeleton of *Tarbosaurus bataar*, a giant tyrannosaur.

The seashore

The coastline of the world

If all the coastlines were straightened out, they would stretch nearly 13 times around the Equator. The total amount of coastline in the world, not counting small bays and inlets, is 504,000 km (313,186 miles).

Beach dunes

Sand dunes on the Atlantic coast of France reach an amazing 91 m (300 ft) high, although beach sand dunes are usually no more than 15 m (50 ft) high. The dunes, blown along by the wind, creep slowly inland, by about 6 m (20 ft) a year, and may bury buildings – and even whole forests.

Stormy weather

On the shores of the northern Pacific Ocean, the force of the waves in winter is equivalent to the impact of a car crashing into a wall at 145 km (90 miles) an hour. Storm waves on the east coast of North America tossed a 61 kg (135 lb) rock 28 m (91 ft) high – on to the roof of a lighthouse.

Skeletons galore!

Corals, which grow in warm, tropical waters, are the skeletons of billions of tiny animals. The Great Barrier Reef is made of coral, and stretches in a series of islands and reefs for 2,028 km (1,260 miles) along the north-east coast of Australia. The Reef has taken at least 12 million years to grow.

Rising tide

On the shore, the sea rises and falls twice a day, at high and low tides. The difference between high and low tide levels ranges from 12 m (40 ft) on some British and Alaskan coasts, to only 30 cm (1 ft) on the Gulf of Mexico coast. The greatest tide is in the Bay of Fundy, eastern Canada, which rises an enormous 16 m (53 ft). The Mediterranean Sea barely has a tide at all.

DID YOU KNOW?

The highest sea cliffs are on the north coast of Moloka'i, Hawaii – a towering 1,005 m (3,300 ft) high. That is about the same height as a 275-storey building.

Sand between the toes

Sand is worn down rock, washed down to the sea by rivers, or made by waves battering and grinding down rocky cliffs. A few beaches have some desert sand, such as those on the Mediterranean Sea, where sand has been blown by the wind across from the Sahara Desert. Some beaches have sand of all one colour, such as the beaches of black lava on Tahiti. Other beaches are a mixture of colours, made from different types of rock, or from worn down coral or seashells. These are some of the sand colours.

Colour	Made of
Black	Lava
Grey	Granite, feldspar
Light brown/tan	Granite, quartz
Yellow	Quartz
Gold	Mica
Red	Garnet
Pink	Feldspar
White	Coral, seashells, quartz

Rock carving

Coastlines are always changing. On rocky shores, the waves pound against the cliffs, flinging up boulders, pebbles and sand. These grind away the rock, forming bays, caves and arches. The top of an arch may collapse, leaving a sea stack, such as the 137 m (450 ft) tall Old Man of Hoy, off the Orkney Islands.

The waves can act as a huge saw, cutting away the softer rock at the foot of a cliff, so that part of the cliff collapses. The lighthouse on the coast at Martha's Vineyard, Massachusetts, USA, has had to be moved 3 times. The waves wear away about 1.7 m (5.5 ft) of the cliff every year.

Mangrove swamps

Enormous mangrove swamps grow in shallow waters on some shores in tropical regions, such as around the mouth of the Ganges River in India. Some mangrove swamps can stretch for 97 km (60 miles) or more inland. The mangrove trees can reach 25 m (82 ft) tall, and have curious stilt-like roots, which prop up the trees.

The changing shore

The level of the sea on the seashore can change over long periods of time. Many of the Ancient Roman ports around the Mediterranean Sea, such as Caesarea on the coast of Israel, are now drowned. In contrast, on Romney Marshes, in Kent, England, the old port of Rye is now over 3 km (2 miles) inland.

The sea

The blue planet

Saltwater covers nearly 70 per cent of the surface of the Earth. The continents and islands divide all that water into the Pacific, Atlantic, Indian and Arctic Oceans – but the four oceans form one continuous expanse of water.

The oceans		
Name	Size, excluding major seas	Average depth
Pacific Ocean	165,384,000 sq km	4,000 m
Atlantic Ocean	82,217,000 sq km	3,300 m
Indian Ocean	73,481,000 sq km	3,800 m
Arctic Ocean	13,986,000 sq km	1,500 m

The largest ocean, the Pacific, covers nearly one-third of the Earth's surface. At its widest point, between Panama and Malaysia, the Pacific stretches 17,700 km (11,000 miles) – nearly halfway around the world.

DID YOU KNOW?

Sound can travel through water at (1,507 in 14,954 ft) a second. That is about 5 times faster than sound travelling through air – 331 m (1,087 ft) a second.

Saltwater

Saltwater contains over 96 per cent pure water and nearly 3 per cent common salt. More than 80 other elements, including gold, make up the rest. These nine substances are found in the greatest quantity.

Sulphate
Magnesium
Calcium
Potassium
Bicarbonate

Bromide
Boron
Strontium
Fluoride

Drinking the sea

When saltwater freezes, the ice contains little or no salt. People living in polar regions, such as Eskimos, can melt the ice – and use it as fresh drinking water.

Tsunamis

Tsunamis, often wrongly called tidal waves, are huge waves caused either by an underwater volcanic explosion or by an earthquake.

One tsunami, triggered by an earthquake, took just over 4½ hours, to travel a distance of 3,220 km (2,000 miles) – from the Aleutian Trench under the north Pacific to Honolulu, in the mid Pacific. The tsunami hit the island with waves more than 15 m (50 ft) high.

Oceans and seas

Each ocean is divided into different areas – the main part, called by the ocean name, and various seas. The seas are mostly around the coasts of the continents and islands. These are the largest seas in each of the oceans.

Ocean	Name of sea	Size
Pacific	Coral	4,790,000 sq km
	South China	3,680,000 sq km
Atlantic	Caribbean	2,750,000 sq km
	Mediterranean	2,510,000 sq km
Indian	Red	450,000 sq km
	Persian Gulf	240,000 sq km
Arctic	Hudson Bay	1,230,000 sq km
	Baffin Bay	690,000 sq km

Hot and cold water

The surface of the sea varies in temperature. The warm, tropical currents can be as hot as 30°C (86°F), the polar currents can be as cold as −2°C (29°F). In the north Atlantic, where the warm Gulf Stream meets the cold Labrador Current, there is a 12°C (22°F) difference in temperature.

Sailing clockwise

The water in the seas is constantly moving around the Earth, flowing in great currents, like rivers in the sea. The currents may be as wide as 80 km (50 miles) and flow at up to 6 km (4 miles) an hour.

The currents in the southern hemisphere mostly swirl anti-clockwise; those in the northern hemisphere swirl in a clockwise direction. In 1492, Columbus sailed from Spain to the West Indies along two currents, the Canaries and the North Equatorial.

Amazing But True

If all the salt was taken out of the seas and spread over the land surface of the Earth, there would be a layer of salt 152 m (500 ft) thick.

Salty seas

The amount of salt in seawater varies. The Red Sea, in the Near East, has almost six times as much salt as the Baltic Sea, in Europe.

Icelandic warmth

The warm Gulf Stream flows from the Caribbean eastwards across the Atlantic Ocean and on past Iceland as far as northern Europe. The winds blowing across the Gulf Stream keep Reyjavik, in Iceland, warmer in winter than New York City, USA 3,862 km (2,400 miles) further south, where there are winds blowing from the cold Labrador Current.

Under the sea

The ocean floor

The ocean floor is not completely flat – there are volcanoes, mountains, valleys and plains, just as there are on dry land.

The ocean plains are solid rock, covered in places in a layer of sand, gravel, clay, silt, or ooze – the remains of countless billions of sea creatures. On average, the layer is 30 m (100 ft) thick; on the floor of the Mediterranean Sea, it is 2,000 m (6,500 ft) thick.

DID YOU KNOW?

The deeper under the sea you go, the greater the pressure, that is the weight of the water above you. At a depth of 9,100 m (30,000 ft), the pressure is equivalent to a 1 tonne weight balanced on a postage stamp.

Undersea mountains

There are mountains in every ocean – together, they form a chain over 60,000 km (37,284 miles) long. In the Pacific Ocean alone there are 14,000 sea mountains, their peaks 610-1,829 m (2,000-6,000 ft) below the surface. Other sea mountains are so huge, they poke through the surface as chains of islands. This map shows the underwater mountain chains.

Pacific Ocean

Atlantic Ocean

Flashlight fish

Many fish living 3,000 m (9,842 ft) down in the dark ocean waters, have their own lights, which are made by bacteria inside the fish. The bacteria glow all the time, but the fish can "switch" the lights off and on.

The angler fish has a bulb of bacteria light at the end of a long spine, which hangs over the fish's mouth. The light attracts other fish – which are gobbled up by the angler.

Light and dark

In the muddy waters off the shores, the water is clear for only about 15 m (50 ft) down. Out in the open ocean, it is clear down to about 110 m (360 ft), and some sunlight can reach 244 m (800 ft) deep. Below that level, it is dark, still – and cold. Deep water is about 3.8°C (39°F), which is close to freezing all the year round.

Diving records

Type of dive		Greatest depth
Breath-held dive		105 m
Scuba dive		133 m
Helmeted diver		176 m
Bathysphere		923 m
Bathyscaphe (*Trieste*)		10,917 m

Deepest dive

Explorers, inside the bathyscaphe *Trieste*, have dived almost to the bottom of the Mariana Trench, the deepest point on Earth. The Trench, south-west of Guam in the Pacific Ocean, plunges to a depth of 11,033 m (36,198 ft) below sea level.

Fishy depths

Different plants and animals live at different depths in the oceans. Floating on the surface, mostly around the coasts and in tropical seas, are billions of tiny plants and animals, called plankton.

Fish living near the surface are often blue, green or violet.

Plants can grow to a depth of about 107 m (350 ft).

Herring

Seaweed **Squid**

107 m (350 ft)

Hatchet fish

Tuna

180 m (600 ft)

Lantern fish

Mackerel

In the twilight zone, 180 m (600 ft) down, fish are silver or light-coloured.

Jellyfish

Great white shark

Deep-sea eel

Deep-sea prawns

457 m (1,500 ft)

In the dark depths, fish are mostly brown, black and deep violet. There are some bright scarlet deep-sea prawns.

Gulper

Amazing But True

Huge worms, 3 m (10 ft) long, blind crabs and giant white clams survive 2,400 m (8,000 ft) down in the darkness of the Pacific Ocean, off the coast of South America. They live near a crack in the ocean floor, where hot mineral-rich water gushes out, providing them with food.

Poles apart

The Arctic Ocean

The Arctic is the smallest of the four oceans, and is less than one-tenth the size of the Pacific, the largest ocean.

Arctic Circle
Arctic Ocean
North Pole
Greenland

Greenland ice sheet statistics	
Area of ice sheet	1,479,000 sq km
Volume of ice	2,800,000 cu km
Thickness of ice	1.6-3 km
Temperature	
July	over 10°C
December	−50°C
Average	−20°C

Arctic Ocean statistics	
Total area	13,986,000 sq km
Area of floating ice	12,000,000 sq km
Average depth of water	1,500 m
Thickness of pack ice	0.6-7.43 m
Coldest water temperature	−51°C

Greenland

About 85 per cent of Greenland is covered by an ice sheet, stretching 2,400 km (1,491 miles) from north to south and up to 1,100 km (683 miles) east to west. The ice sheet is 7½ times the size of Britain. The 50,000 people on the island can only live on the coasts.

Slow-growing plants

Some Arctic lichens may be over 4,500 years old, and have taken hundreds of years to grow 2.5 cm (1 in).

All that ice

The polar ice sheets hold just over 2 per cent of all the Earth's water. If all the ice melted, the sea level around the world would rise by about 60 m (200 ft). Many coastal areas would be drowned, including major cities such as London, Tokyo and New York.

Hunt the seal

In the Arctic, seals spend much of their time under water, but need to come up for air about every 20 minutes. When the seas are frozen, the seals chew several big breathing holes in the ice.

Polar bears hunt seals, and wait on the ice by a breathing hole. When the seal comes up, the polar bear grabs it.

Midnight Sun

As the Earth travels around the Sun, one of the Poles is always facing towards it. The North Pole has continuous daylight from mid-March to mid-September. From mid-September to mid-March, it is the South Pole's turn for continuous daylight.

Antarctica

Nearly one-tenth of the Earth's surface is permanently covered in ice. About 90 per cent of all that ice is in the ice sheets of Antarctica and Greenland. The other 10 per cent is in mountain glaciers.

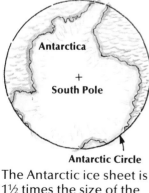

The Antarctic ice sheet is 1½ times the size of the USA, and has nine times more ice than the Greenland ice sheet.

Antarctic wildlife

Insects, 13 mm (0.5 in) long, are the only creatures living all the time on Antarctica itself. The wildlife lives in the seas and islands around the coast, including the blue whale, the largest creature on Earth, 30 m (98 ft) long and 136 tonnes in weight.

Penguins live on the islands. Scientists think that Adelie penguins might use the Sun to navigate back to their nests from up to 3,058 km (1,900 miles) away. Penguins can "fly" underwater at 40 km (25 miles) an hour.

DID YOU KNOW?

There is no land at the North Pole – it is a floating raft of ice. In 1958, *Nautilus,* the US submarine, was the first to cross the Arctic Ocean – a distance of 2,945 km (1,830 miles) – by travelling underneath the North Pole.

Volcano

There is still one active volcano in Antarctica. Mount Erebus, in the Transantarctic Range, reaches up 4,900 m (16,075 ft) above the ice. Erebus steams and spouts ash, even though it is covered in snow.

Antarctica statistics	
Area of ice sheet	13,000,000 sq km
Volume of ice sheet	29,000,000 cu km
Thickness of ice	3-4 km
Area of sea ice	
March	3,000,000 sq km
September	22,000,000 sq km
Average thickness of sea ice	4 m
Temperature	
Interior average	−50°C
Coastal average	−20°C

Icebergs and glaciers

Icing

Glaciers cover 10½ per cent of the Earth's land surface, an area equal to the size of South America. Glaciers contain enough ice to cover the entire Earth with a layer of ice, 30 m (98 ft) thick.

Glacier lengths

Name	Location	Length
Lambert/Fisher Ice Passage	Antarctica	515 km
Novaya Zemlya Glacier	USSR	418 km
Arctic Institute Ice Passage	Antarctica	362 km
Nimrod/Lennox/King Ice Passage	Antarctica	289 km
Denman Glacier	Antarctica	241 km
Beardmore Glacier	Antarctica	225 km
Recovery Glacier	Antarctica	225 km
Petermanns Gletscher Glacier	Greenland	200 km
Unnamed Glacier	Antarctica	193 km

Glaciers on the move

Glaciers creep down mountains at a rate of between 2.5-60 cm (1-24 in) a day. A few glaciers move much faster, such as two on Greenland: up to 24 m (79 ft) a day for the Quarayag Glacier and 28 m (92 ft) for the Rinks Isbrae Glacier.

Busy glacier

The Jakobshavn Isbrae Glacier in Greenland moves at about 7 km (4 miles) a year. Every day, over 142 million tonnes of ice break off and float away as 1,500 or so icebergs each year.

DID YOU KNOW?

At least 75 per cent of all the freshwater on Earth is deep frozen inside glaciers. That amount of water would equal non-stop rain all over the Earth for as much as 60 years.

Tropical glaciers

Glaciers and snowfields are found near the Equator, on mountains which are over 6,000 m (20,000 ft) high. There is glacier ice 61 m (200 ft) deep in the Kibo Peak crater on Mount Kilimanjaro in Tanzania.

Deep ice

A depth of glacier ice as thick as 4,330 m (14,206 ft) has been recorded on Byrd Station in Antarctica. Most glaciers are between 91-3,000 m (299-9,842 ft) deep.

Crevasse

Crevasses, cracks in glaciers, can be 40 m (131 ft) deep. The bodies of climbers who fell into a crevasse in the Bossons Glacier on Mont Blanc in the Alps in 1820, were not found until 1861, when they reached the melting "snout", the end of the glacier.

An Arctic iceberg drifted about 4,000 km (2,486 miles), nearly as far south as the island of Bermuda. An Antarctic iceberg drifted about 5,500 km (3,418 miles), nearly as far north as Rio de Janeiro, in Brazil.

Biggest berg

The largest iceberg ever recorded, off the coast of Antarctica, was 335 km (208 miles) long and 97 km (60 miles) wide. It covered an area of 31,000 sq km (12,000 sq miles), about the same size as Belgium.

Hidden depth

Only about one-tenth of an iceberg floats above the surface. If there is 122 m (400 ft) above the water, then there must be as much as 1,098 m (3,600 ft) below the water.

Icy heights

The tallest iceberg ever recorded, off west Greenland, was 167 m (550 ft) high. That is more than half as tall as the Eiffel Tower in Paris, France.

Iceberg ahoy!

The International Ice Patrol keeps track of all icebergs, and warns ships of any possible danger. The Patrol was set up after the giant liner, the *Titanic*, sank after hitting an iceberg on the night of 14 April 1912: 1,490 people drowned out of a total of 2,201 passengers and crew.

Watering the desert

Icebergs are made of freshwater and could be used to supply water in desert areas. Scientists think that tugs could be built, which could tow large icebergs at a rate of 400 km (250 miles) a day.

The journey from Antarctica to western Australia might take 107-150 days, and to the Atacama Desert in Chile 145-200 days. Only about half of each iceberg would melt on the way.

Long-life bergs

Satellites can track the lives of icebergs. The Trolltunga iceberg in Antarctica was tracked for 11 years, until it broke up into several smaller bergs. At up to 25 km (15½ miles) a day, icebergs can travel a total distance of as much as 2,500 km (1,550 miles).

Earthquakes

Earthquake areas

Earthquakes happen under the sea as well as on land. Ninety per cent occur in the "ring of fire", which circles the Pacific Ocean. Many others occur along the Alpine Belt, which stretches from Spain to Turkey, and on through the Himalayas as far as South-East Asia.

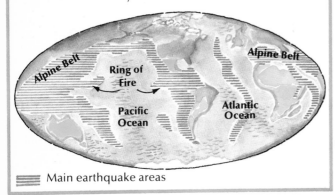

Alpine Belt
Ring of Fire
Alpine Belt
Pacific Ocean
Atlantic Ocean

Main earthquake areas

Disaster area

China, on the Alpine Belt of earthquakes, has the worst record for earthquake deaths. In 1556, an earthquake killed 830,000 people in Shanxi province. In 1976, the earthquake in Tangshan province – 8.2 on the Richter Scale – killed 750,000 people.

Danger!

Animals, such as dogs and chickens, some people believe, can sense faint vibrations or smells and warn people that an earthquake might happen. In 1975, in Haicheng, China, thousands of people escaped an earthquake because they were warned of the danger.

Magnitude

The magnitude, that is the power, of an earthquake is measured on the Richter Scale. Starting at 1, each number on the Scale is ten times more powerful than the number below. An earthquake of magnitude 7 is about as powerful as a one megaton nuclear bomb; the worst earthquake so far recorded was 8.9.

A million earthquakes

There are about a million earthquakes every year – any vibration of the Earth's crust is an earthquake. Most are so tiny, they only register on a seismograph, which measures the slightest movement in the crust. A large earthquake occurs about every two weeks – mostly under the sea, where it does little harm.

DID YOU KNOW?

Earthquakes under the sea can trigger off great avalanches of mud and sand. These can cause undersea currents strong enough to snap underwater cables. Telephone cables broke under the Atlantic Ocean, after the earthquake off Newfoundland in 1929.

Splash!

The shock of an earthquake can sometimes be felt hundreds of kilometres away. Water splashed in swimming pools in Houston, USA, after the earthquake in Mexico in 1985 – 1,609 km (1,000 miles) away.

Shocking

An earthquake usually lasts for less than 1 minute. The earthquake in Lisbon, Portugal, in 1755 lasted for 10 minutes, and the shock waves were felt as far away as North Africa.

Rock avalanches

The 1970 earthquake off the coast of Peru caused an avalanche of snow and rock on land – high on the Nevados Huascaran mountain. The avalanche fell 4,000 m (13,123 ft), and buried the town of Yungay under 10 m (33 ft) of rock, killing at least 18,000 people.

Fire! fire!

Huge fires can break out after an earthquake. In 1906, after the earthquake in San Francisco, USA, fire destroyed the wooden buildings of the city. The water pipes had burst, and the fire raged for 3½ days. But within 9 years, the city had been rebuilt.

Amazing But True

The ground can roll like waves on the ocean in a very bad earthquake. The 1964 earthquake in Alaska lasted for 7 minutes. The shaking opened up huge cracks in the ground, up to 90 cm (3 ft) wide and 12 m (40 ft) deep. Many buildings tilted and slid down into the cracks.

Twentieth-century earthquakes

These are some of the most serious earthquakes this century, measured on the Richter Scale.

Date	Location	Richter Scale
1906	Coast of Colombia	8.9
1906	Jammu and Kashmir, India	8.6
1906	Valparaiso, Chile	8.6
1920	Kansu province, China	8.5
1929	Fox Islands, Alaska	8.6
1933	North Honshu, Japan	8.9
1941	Coast of Portugal	8.4
1950	Assam, India	8.3
1960	Lebu, Chile	8.5
1964	Prince William Sound, Alaska	8.5

Volcanoes

Hot spots

There are more than 600 active volcanoes on Earth. About half of these are in the "ring of fire" – on land and under the sea – which circles the Pacific Ocean;

Indonesia alone has about 160 active volcanoes. Many islands are volcanic, such as the Hawaiian islands – and Iceland, which has about 200 active volcanoes.

Iceland

Hawaii

Ring of Fire

Indonesia

Pacific Ocean

Atlantic Ocean

∴∴ Main volcanic areas

Living dangerously

A blanket of ash can cover the countryside when a volcano explodes. But the ash helps make the soil very fertile, and many people risk the danger of living near an active volcano. Three crops of rice a year can be grown on the slopes of Gunung Agung, in Bali, a volcano which exploded in 1963, killing 2,000 people.

Eruptions

On average, between 20-30 volcanoes erupt each year. A few volcanoes erupt more or less all the time, such as the island of Stromboli, Italy, which shoots a shower of glowing ash into the sky every 20 minutes or so. Other volcanoes are dormant; sometimes they do not erupt for tens or hundreds of years. Mount Etna, in Sicily, has erupted about 150 times in the last 3,500 years.

Rivers of fire

Lava is fiery hot molten rock – up to 1200°C (2190°F). On Mount Tolbachik, in the Kamchatka Peninsula, USSR, in 1975, the lava flow gushed out at 168 m (550 ft) a second. And when Laki, in Iceland, exploded in 1782, the hot lava flowed a distance of about 65 km (40 miles).

Hot water

Underground water is heated by the hot rocks in volcanic areas. The water can bubble to the surface as a hot spring, or can spout high in the air as a geyser – a jet of steam and scalding water. Yellowstone Park in the USA has hot springs and 10,000 geysers; Old Faithful Geyser erupts 40 m (130 ft) high every 30-90 minutes.

Glowing clouds

Volcanoes can release clouds of ash, as well as cinders, gases and lava. Ash clouds can flow downhill at 200 km (124 miles) an hour, or can billow upwards. When Mayon, in the Philippines, erupted in 1968, ash and blocks of lava were hurled 600 m (1,968 ft) into the air, and the ash clouds rose to a height of 10 km (6 miles).

Mud avalanches

Some volcanic explosions trigger off a lethal avalanche of mud. When the Nevado del Ruiz, in Colombia, erupted in 1985, the heat melted the ice and snow on the peak. This caused a torrent of mud and water, which destroyed the town of Armero in five minutes, killing 20,000 people.

Major active volcanoes by continent			
Continent	Country	Volcano	Height
Asia	USSR	Kluchevskaya	4,750 m
Africa	Zaire	Nyiragongo	3,520 m
North America	Alaska	My Wrangell	4,270 m
South America	Argentina	Antofalla	6,127 m
Antarctica	Ross Island	Erebus	3,720 m
Europe	Sicily	Etna	3,340 m
Oceania	New Zealand	Ruapehu	2,797 m

DID YOU KNOW?

The largest active volcano on Earth is Mauna Loa, in Hawaii. It is 4,168 m (13,677 ft) high, and one eruption lasted for 1½ years.

Lava tubes

Lava flows can be 20 m (66 ft) thick, and can take several years to cool. Inside some flows are huge tunnels – lava tubes, as much as 10 m (33 ft) high. Hot lava hangs down from the tube roof as lava stalactites, and drips on to the tube floor, forming lava stalagmites.

Krakatoa

The loudest sound ever recorded was the eruption which blew up the island of Krakatoa, near Java, in 1883. The noise was heard in Australia, 4,800 km (3,000 miles) away, and the shock was felt in California, USA, 14,500 km (9,000 miles) away.

Rock and fire blasted 80 km (50 miles) up into the air. The wind carried volcanic dust around the Earth, causing vivid sunsets as far away as London, England. Tsunamis, huge waves 30 m (100 ft) high, crashed 16 km (10 miles) inland on Java and Sumatra, killing 36,000 people.

Natural resources

What are natural resources?

Many resources from the Earth provide light and heat, such as oil, coal and gas from under the ground, and firewood and charcoal from trees. And hot water and steam can be piped up from under the ground.

The power of the water in rivers, and the speed of the wind, are used to generate electricity. And sunlight is collected in solar panels and cells, to heat water and supply electricity.

Will natural resources last forever?

The supply of fossil fuels, that is oil, coal and gas, which were formed millions of years ago, will run out one day. At the rate we are burning them at present, scientists think that oil and gas may be used up in 70 years' time, and coal in 300 years' time. But there may be more supplies in the ground and under the sea which have not yet been found.

Oil rig

Twenty per cent of the world's oil comes from wells beneath the sea. One North Sea oil rig can produce up to 320,000 litres (70,400 gallons) of oil a day. At an average of 55 litres (12 gallons) each, that would fill the petrol tanks of 5,800 cars.

Coal supply

Coal was mined by the Romans as long ago as the 1st century AD. But there is still a huge amount of coal in the ground. These countries have the biggest reserves of coal.

USSR	UK
USA	Poland
China	Australia
West Germany	

DID YOU KNOW?

Only 5.5 per cent of the world's population live in the USA. But they use nearly 29 per cent of the world's petrol and nearly 33 per cent of the world's electricity.

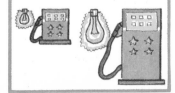

Sources of energy

These are the major natural resources that are used for energy on Earth today.

Source of energy		Per cent
🌢🌢🌢🌢🌢	Oil	39
🪨🪨🪨🪨🪨	Coal	27
🌰🌰🌰🌰🌰🌰	Gas	17
🌳🌳🌳🌳	Fuelwood/charcoal	12
〰️〰️〰️	Hydro (water) power	2
⛲⛲⛲⛲	Other, such as underground heat and hot water springs	2
🏭🏭🏭🏭	Nuclear power	1

River power

The force of flowing water in rivers and over waterfalls is used to generate nearly one-quarter of the world's electricity. These are some of the countries using water power to make their electricity.

Country	Per cent
Norway	100
Brazil	93
Switzerland	79
Canada	70
France	50
Italy	50
Japan	30
West Germany	20
USA	20
USSR	20

Boiling water

Hot water is piped from under the ground in Iceland, and used to heat homes, factories – and outdoor swimming pools. The capital city, Reykjavik, is supplied with 250 litres (55 gallons) of boiling water every second.

Products from fossil fuels

Many products are made from coal and oil. These are just a few examples.

Products from coal

Plastics
Heavy chemicals
Perfumes
Insectides
Antiseptics
Road surfaces
Coal gas

Products from oil

Petrol (gasoline)
Kerosene (jet fuel)
Diesel fuel
Paraffin wax
Pharmaceuticals
Explosives
Pesticides
Detergents
Cosmetics
Adhesives
Polishes
Paints
Nylon
Plastics

Using the Sun

Solar panels in the roofs of houses trap the heat from the Sun. Many homes in Israel, Canada, Australia and Japan have solar panels. Panels covering as little as 3 sq m (32 sq ft) can heat as much as 226 litres (50 gallons) of water a day – enough for 2 baths and all the washing up.

Rocks, minerals and metals

The rocks of the Earth's crust

The Earth's crust is made up of different kinds of rocks. They all belong to one of the 3 rock families, which are called igneous, sedimentary and metamorphic. These are some examples of the different families.

Igneous rocks

Igneous rocks are made from hot, molten rock, deep inside the Earth's mantle.

Granite
Hard, coarse-grained rock

Basalt
Hard, fine-grained rock

Obsidian
Black or greenish volcanic glass

Sedimentary rocks

Sedimentary rocks are layers made from worn fragments of rock, and may contain the remains of plants and animals.

Limestone
Hard rock; often contains lots of shells

Chalk
Soft rock; contains remains of small animals and shells

Sandstone
Formed from beach, river or desert sands

Metamorphic rocks

Metamorphic rocks are made from rocks which are pushed back down in the mantle, where they change under heat and pressure into different rocks.

Slate
Formed under high pressure from shale

Marble
Formed under heat from different limestones

Quartzite
Formed under heat and high pressure from sandstone

Minerals

The rocks of the Earth's crust contain a mixture of over 2,000 minerals. But about 90 per cent of the crust is made up of just 20 minerals, such as mica, quartz and feldspar. These are the uses of some minerals.

Mineral	Use
Graphite	Lead pencil
Gypsum	School chalk
Silica	Glass, mirrors
Potassium	Fertilizers
Sodium	
Fluorite	Toothpaste
Cobalt	Blue colouring
Sodium chloride	Household salt

Amazing But True

Pumice, a kind of lava, is full of gas bubbles, and is light enough to float on water – the only rock to do so.

Elementary!

Rocks are a mixture of one or more minerals. Minerals are made up of chemical elements. These are the chemical elements found in the greatest quantity in the Earth's crust.

Name of element	Per cent
Oxygen	46.60
Silicon	27.72
Aluminium	8.13
Iron	5.00
Calcium	3.63
Sodium	2.82
Potassium	2.59
Magnesium	2.09 = 98.6%
Titanium	0.44
Hydrogen	0.14
Phosphorus	0.12
Manganese	0.10
Fluorine	0.08
Sulphur	0.05
Chlorine	0.04
Carbon	0.03 = 1.0%
Others, including gold and silver	0.41 = 0.4%

Sparklers

About 100 minerals, because of their beauty and rarity, are known as gemstones, such as diamonds and sapphires. Emeralds and rubies are the most valuable gems; they are the rarest.

DID YOU KNOW?

Minerals are graded according to their hardness, on a scale from 1 to 10. Talc, used as talcum powder, is the softest mineral, rated 1; quartz rates 7. Diamond is rated 10 – the hardest mineral on Earth. Only a diamond can be used to cut and polish another diamond.

Diamond bright

Diamonds are found in a rainbow of colours – white, yellow, pink, green, blue, brown, red and black. In the ground, they usually look like dull, rounded pebbles – they only glitter and shine once they have been cut and polished. The small and badly-coloured diamonds are used in cutting tools.

Metalwork

Many of the metals in the rocks of the Earth's crust, such as silver, tin, mercury, iron and lead, have been mined for thousands of years. In the Middle East, 8,000 years ago, copper and gold were used for making jewellery. The gold mask of the Pharaoh Tutankhamun was made over 3,000 years ago.

Gold diggers

Miners today have to dig as much as 2 tonnes (2 tons) of rock to find only 28 grams (1 oz) of gold. If the 50 million tonnes of waste rock from just one South African gold mine were spread out, the rock would bury Manhattan island, New York, USA, under a layer 2.4 m (8 ft) deep.

39

Changing the world

The people on Earth

The Earth has a limited amount of oil and coal, wood and soil. People are using up these natural resources at an alarming rate, as well as spoiling the landscape and polluting the water and air – and may be changing the future of the Earth.

Croplands

Trees and hedges have been dug up to make enormous fields. One cornfield in the American Midwest can be 810 hectares (2,000 acres) in size. This makes harvesting the crops easier. But growing the same crop every year makes the soil less fertile and the harvest becomes smaller each year. And pests can destroy whole fields of crops.

Deserts

The deserts of the world are growing bigger, taking over the farmland at the edges, because of creeping sand dunes. The Sahara Desert alone is expanding southwards at an average of 0.8 km (½ mile) a month.

Water pollution

Chemical waste from factories is dumped or washed into seas, lakes and rivers, where it kills fish and plants. The Mediterranean Sea is one of the most polluted areas of water on Earth. In some places, the surface is now covered with a thin film of oil spilled from ships, and it is not safe to swim.

The changing climate

Some scientists think that burning coal and oil, and burning tropical forests, might lead to a change in the weather – the Earth might grow warmer, by as much as 7°C (12.5°F) at the Poles. This would melt some of the ice, and sea levels could rise by up to 7 m (23 ft), drowning all the ports.

Other scientists think that the dust produced by burning coal, oil and wood could block out some of the Sun's rays. The Earth might become colder – great sheets of ice could cover the northern hemisphere at least as far south as London, England.

Farmland

Only 11 per cent of the Earth's land is used for farming. But each year, less and less land can be used for growing crops and grazing cattle because the soil is washed away by the rain or blown away by the wind.

In the 1930s, farmers in the American Southwest ploughed up the plains to grow wheat. But as much as 25 cm (10 in) of soil was blown away by the wind – creating the Dust Bowl, where no plants could grow.

DID YOU KNOW?

Every year, the amount of trees cut down could cover a city the size of Birmingham, England, with a pile of wood, ten storeys high.

Vanishing forest

Forests cover just over a quarter of the Earth. But every year, forests the size of England, Scotland and Wales are cut down or spoilt. By the year 2000, one-third of all the tropical forests may have been destroyed.

Too much traffic

The exhaust fumes from cars, buses and trucks can poison the air. More than one-third of West Germany's Black Forest is dying, probably from the effect of these fumes. Cities, such as Los Angeles, USA and Tokyo, Japan, are often covered with a thick, choking smog. This is caused by the reaction of exhaust fumes and sunlight.

Acid rain

Factories and power stations burning oil and coal put huge amounts of poisonous gases and chemicals into the air. These combine with rain and snow and can fall hundreds of kilometres away, destroying forests and killing all the life in lakes.

Carried by the wind, pollution from British factories has killed many of the fish and plants in 18,000 lakes in Sweden. And more than half the pollution which falls on Canada comes from the USA.

Mining

Mining for minerals, such as bauxite, can destroy vast areas of land, and can cause pollution. Waste from copper mining in Malaysia has been washed into rivers, poisoning the fish.

The Earth's future

The people on Earth

Over the centuries, people have made great changes to the Earth – many of them bad. But people are now trying to do something to look after the soil, recycle rubbish and help stop some of the air and water pollution.

Cleaning up

Polluted lakes and rivers can be cleaned up. Filters fitted to power stations can remove some of the gases pouring into the air, or some of the gases can be treated and turned into fertilizer. Fish now swim in the River Thames, once one of the most polluted rivers in Europe, because factory wastes are treated and not dumped in the river.

Terracing

Heavy rain can wash the soil away on steep mountain slopes. Building terraces holds back the soil, and crops can be grown. There are terraces in Bali, where three crops of rice can be grown each year.

Pest control

In parts of China, ducks are used instead of pesticides to control insect pests in rice fields. In the Big Sand commune, thousands of ducks eat about 200 insects each an hour. This system has another advantage, because rain can wash the pesticide off the fields into lakes and rivers, where it pollutes the water.

Saving water

Spraying crops with water in dry areas is very wasteful because so much is lost in evaporation. Huge amounts of water can be saved by giving plants small measured amounts of water, through holes in thin plastic tubes. In Israel, computers control when to turn the water off and on and when to give the plants fertilizer.

Looking after the soil

The soil can be made more fertile by growing different crops together, rather than growing only one crop. In Java, pineapples and winged beans are grown in alternate rows, which keeps the soil fertile.

Tree planting

More trees are being planted, to supply wood for industry, and fuel for heating and cooking. In South Korea, where most of the wood is used for fuel, 70 per cent of the country has now been planted with young trees. And in Gujarat, India, school children are planting tree seedlings, to provide wood for heating and cooking.

Recycling rubbish

Rubbish can be sorted and recycled. Over half the aluminium drinks cans in the USA are melted down and recycled. In Britain, glass bottles are sorted into different colours, melted and reused.

Planting the desert

Expanding deserts can be stopped by planting bushes at the edges to hold back the sand dunes. And the bushes can be used for crops too – jojoba produces liquid wax, and guayule and a type of dandelion can produce latex, which is used as rubber.

Farming the wind

Electricity can be generated by windmills – rather than by power stations which burn oil or coal. Fields full of windmills could supply 8 per cent of electricity in California, USA by the year 2000. A wind "farm", with about 4,600 windmills, can supply as many as 30,000 homes with electricity.

Saving coal and oil

Using rubbish for fuel saves oil or coal. In Edmonton, England, electricity is generated by burning about 2 per cent of Britain's total rubbish, saving about 100,000 tonnes of coal each year.

Saving trees

About 35 million trees could be saved each year, if 75 per cent of waste paper and cardboard was recycled into pulp and used to make new paper.

DID YOU KNOW?

A quarter of all the cars in Brazil run on fuel made from sugar cane, and half the cars in South Africa use fuel made from liquid coal.

43

Earth map

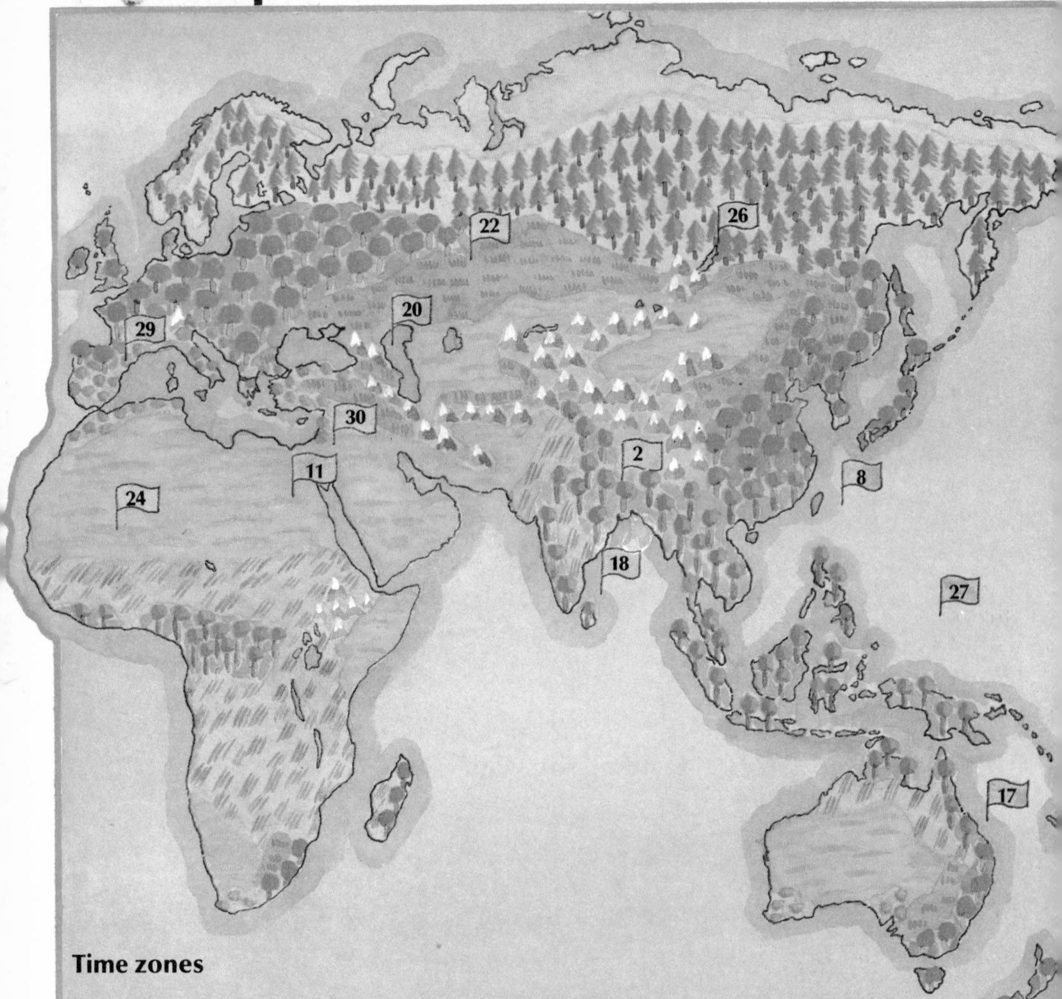
22
26
20
29
30
2
11
8
24
18
27
17

Time zones

When it is daytime in Britain, it is nighttime in Australia, because the Earth is divided into different time zones – based on the time at Greenwich, London, England. These are the times around the world, when it is 12.00 noon in London.

London, England

Moscow, USSR

Dacca, Bangladesh

Tokyo, Japan

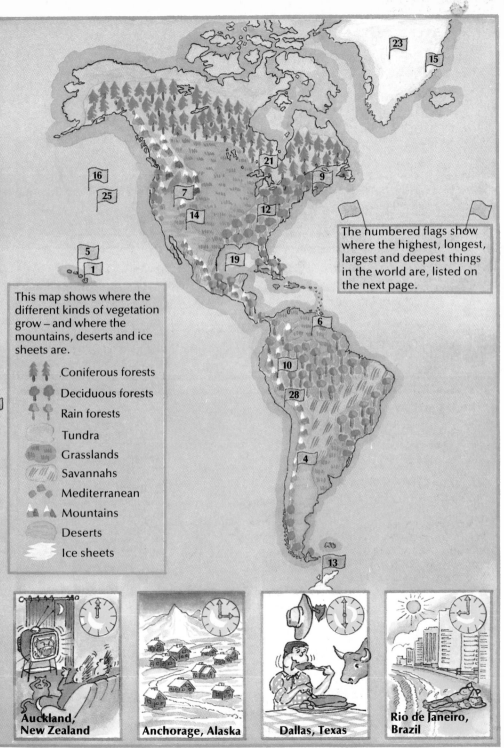

The numbered flags show where the highest, longest, largest and deepest things in the world are, listed on the next page.

This map shows where the different kinds of vegetation grow – and where the mountains, deserts and ice sheets are.

Coniferous forests
Deciduous forests
Rain forests
Tundra
Grasslands
Savannahs
Mediterranean
Mountains
Deserts
Ice sheets

Auckland, New Zealand

Anchorage, Alaska

Dallas, Texas

Rio de Janeiro, Brazil

The Earth in a nutshell

The highest . . .

1 Mountain on Earth
Mauna Kea, Hawaii
10,023 m measured from
the sea floor

2 Mountain on land
Mount Everest, Nepal/Tibet
8,843 m

3 Mountain under the sea
Near Tonga Trench, Tonga
Islands, Pacific Ocean
8,690 m

4 Active volcano
Antofalla, Argentina
6,127 m

5 Sea cliffs
Umilehi Point, Moloka'i,
Hawaii
1,005 m

6 Waterfall
Angel Falls, Venezuela
979 m

7 Active geyser
Service Steamboat Geyser,
Yellowstone, USA
Maximum 115 m

8 Tsunami
Ishigaki Island, Japan
85 m

9 Tide
Bay of Fundy, Nova Scotia,
Canada
Range of 14.5 m

The longest . . .

10 Mountain range
Andes, South America
7,240 km

11 River
River Nile, Egypt
6,670 km

12 Cave system
Mammoth Cave National
Park, Kentucky, USA
484 km

13 Glacier
Lambert/Mellor, Antarctica
402 km

14 Canyon
Grand Canyon on Colorado
River, Arizona, USA
349 km

15 Fjord
Nordvest Fjord, Greenland
313 km

The largest . . .

16 Ocean
Pacific Ocean
165,384,000 sq km

17 Sea
Coral Sea (part of Pacific
Ocean)
4,790,000 sq km

18 Bay
Bay of Bengal
2,172,000 sq km

19 Gulf
Gulf of Mexico
1,544,000 sq km

20 Inland sea
Caspian Sea, Iran/USSR
372,000 sq km

21 Lake
Lake Superior, Canada/USA
82,414 sq km

22 Continent
Asia
44,391,200 sq km

23 Island
Greenland
2,175,000 sq km

24 Desert
Sahara Desert, North Africa
8,400,000 sq km

The deepest . . .

25 Ocean
Pacific Ocean
Average depth 4,000 m

26 Lake
Lake Baikal, USSR
Maximum 1,940 m

27 Sea trench
Mariana Trench, Pacific
Ocean
11,033 m

28 Canyon
Colca Canyon, Peru
3,223 m

29 Cave
Gouffre Jean Bernard,
France
1,535 m

30 Land below sea level
Dead Sea, Israel/Jordan
395 m

Index

First published in 1986. Usborne Publishing Ltd, Usborne House, 83-85 Saffron Hill, London EC1N 8RT.
Copyright © 1986 Usborne Publishing Ltd. All rights reserved. No part of this publication may be reproduced, stored
in a retrieval system, or transmitted by any means, electronic, mechanical, photocopying, recording, or otherwise,
without the prior permission of the publisher. The name Usborne and the device 😃 are Trade Marks of Usborne
Publishing Ltd. Printed in Belgium.